P9-BZC-087

What Cats Think

Mies van Hout

text by John Spray

pajamapress

I would like to thank the publishers, friends, and family who contributed to the making of this book. I would especially like to thank Monique Postma for her approach, support and insight. —**M.V.H.**

For all my cat friends past and present: Bert, Tony, Tigger, Bear, and Sasha. I knew you could talk…you just chose not to. —**J.S.**

What Cats Think

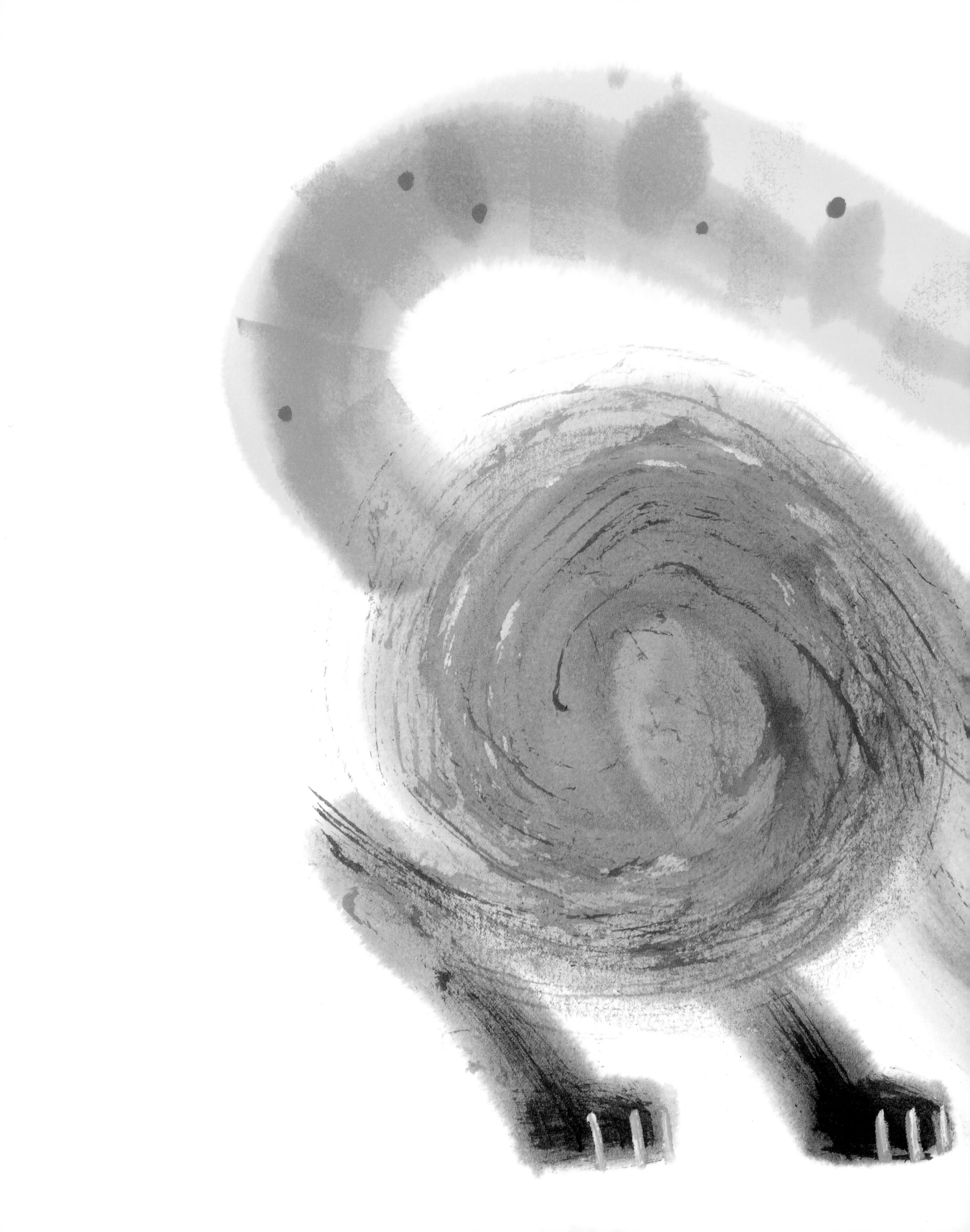

Pamper

Every day I looove to stretch.

...Just like my friend the lady does.

The Kitty-Cat is the best yoga pose.

I am a pampered cat.

Purr...

Vexed

It's raining out, so inside I sit.
At least that girl can color.
My favorite one is bluebird blue.
But my paws can't hold the crayons!

Sigh…

Charmer

Now, watch me do my **cuddly** act,
then tickle my warm belly.
Scratch behind my **silky** ears,
then pet me till I take my nap.

Coo...

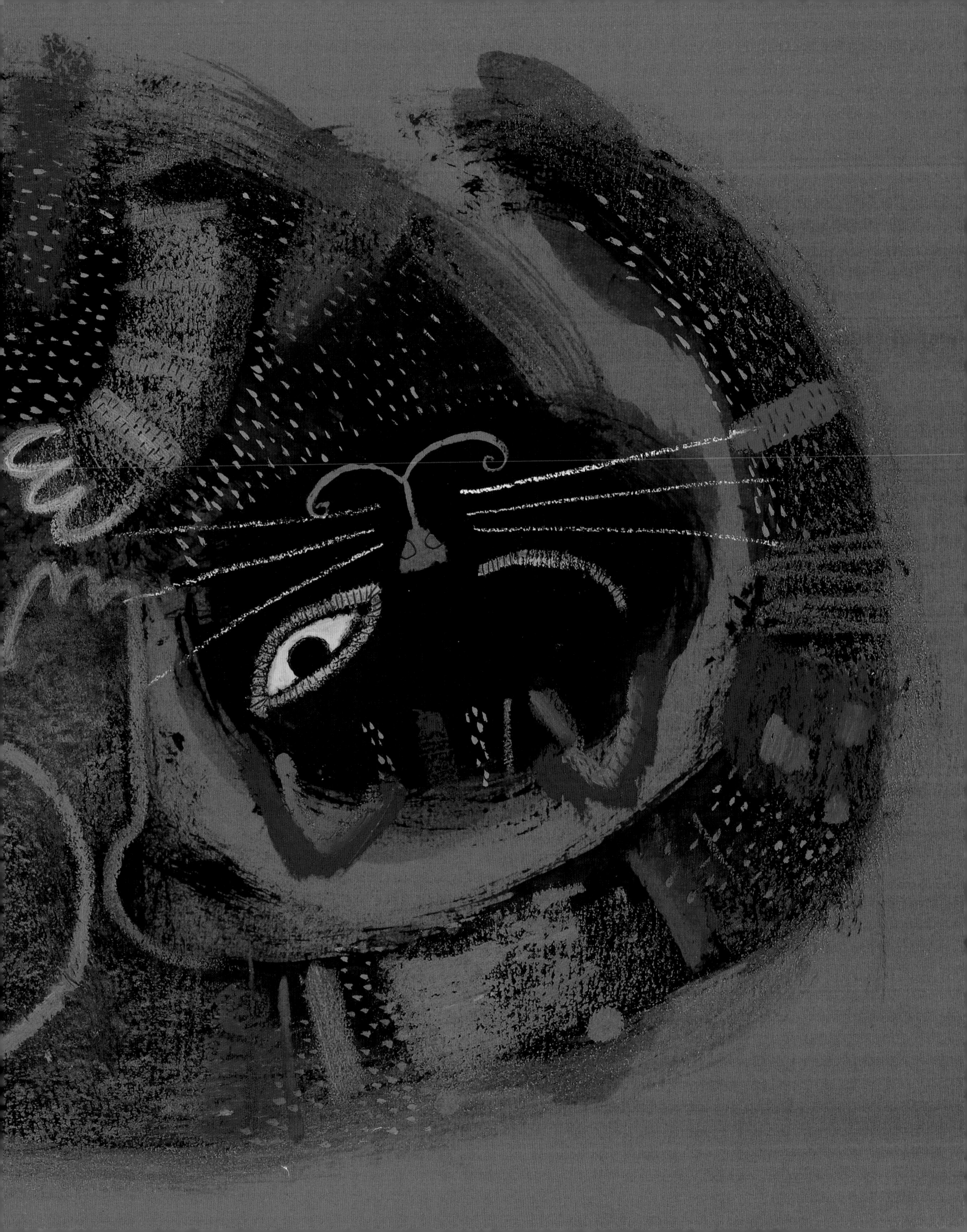

Teasing

THAT bird won't stop twittering.

She flies just out of reach…

…and tweets the same old silly song.

It's NEVER nice to tease!

Harrumph…

Capture

That buzzing fly is back again.

It laughs when I can't catch it.

I wish I had a lizard's tongue...

or big paws like a polar bear!

Pounce.

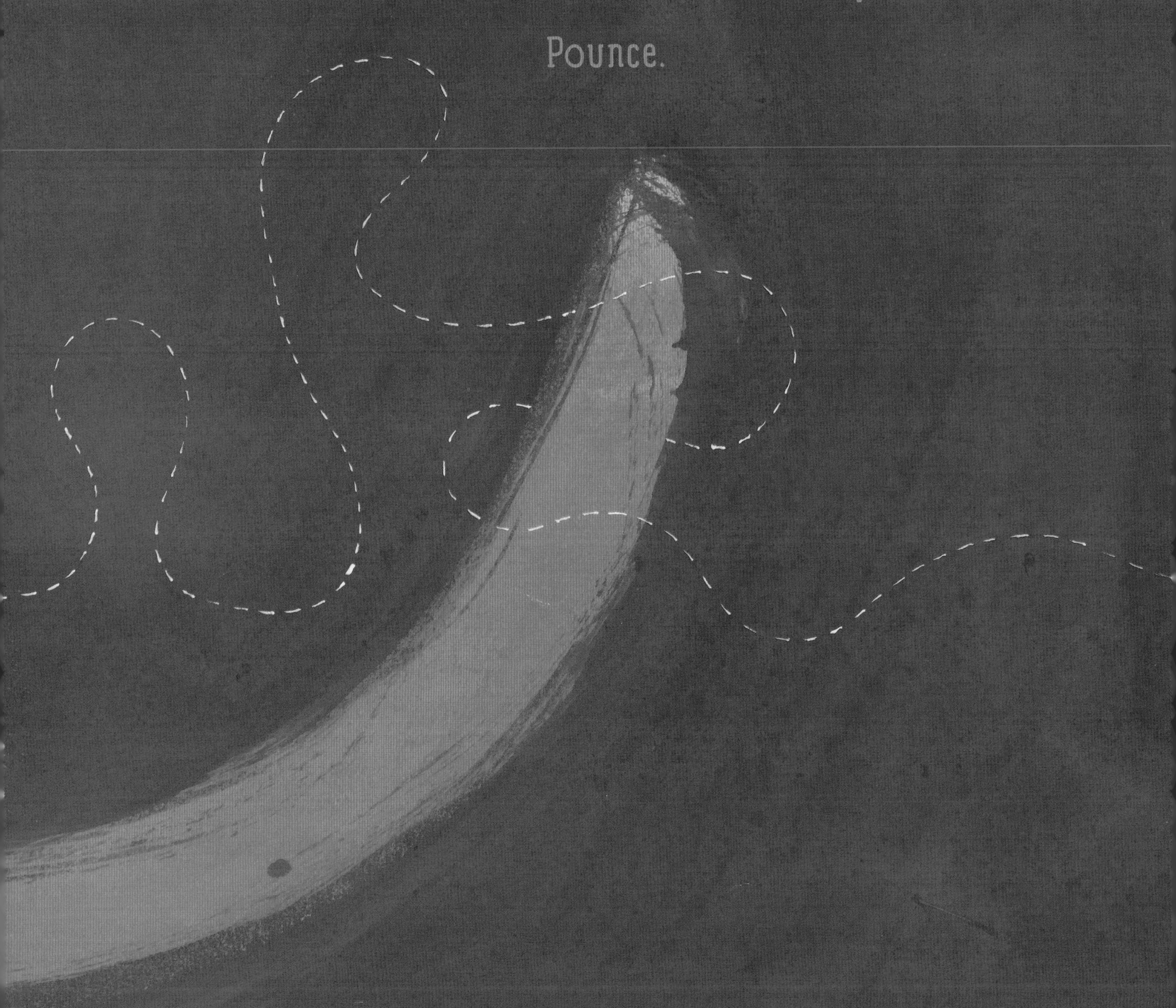

Worry

I saw him getting out the cage.

Now it's off to the kitty vet.

Needles and that thermometer—OUCH!

There'd better be treats later!

Shiver...

Spooked

A THUMP on the front door?
There's a hungry bear on the porch!
There's a growly wolf on the lawn!
Oh. It's just the paperboy.

Phew…

Pouting

Okay, sorry I got on the counter.
But the turkey smelled SO good!
I only had a little taste...
...but they YELLED and chased me away!

Sniffle.

Dream

I close my eyes and dream…

Of saucers filled with steamy milk.

Rivers of creamy moo-cow juice…

…big white waves on milky seas.

Ahhh…only a dream.

Angry

You threw away my **scratching post!**
I know I ripped it up to shreds.
But **that post** was covered in my scent...
...and was a **comfy** friend.

Grr!

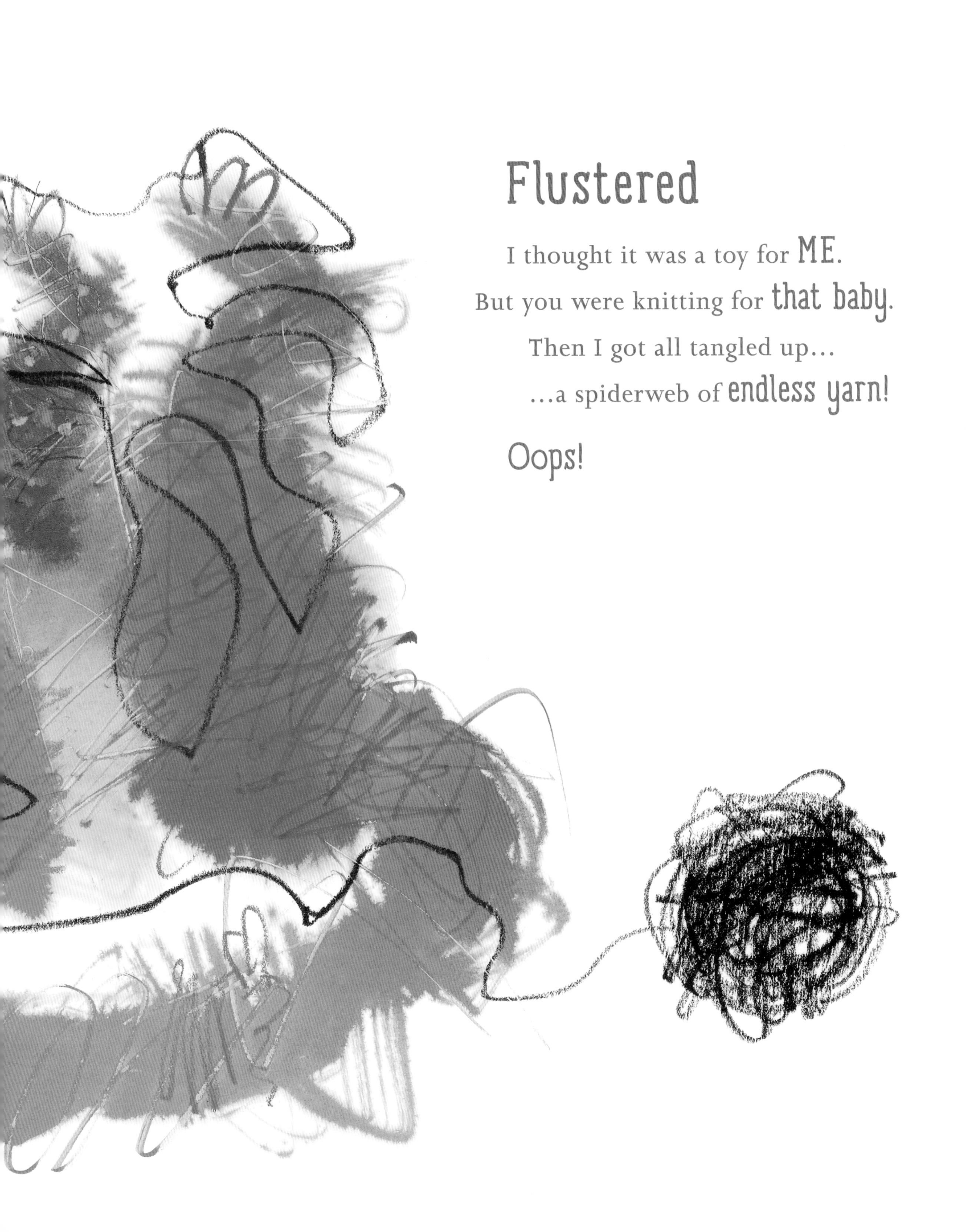

Flustered

I thought it was a toy for ME.

But you were knitting for that baby.

Then I got all tangled up...

...a spiderweb of endless yarn!

Oops!

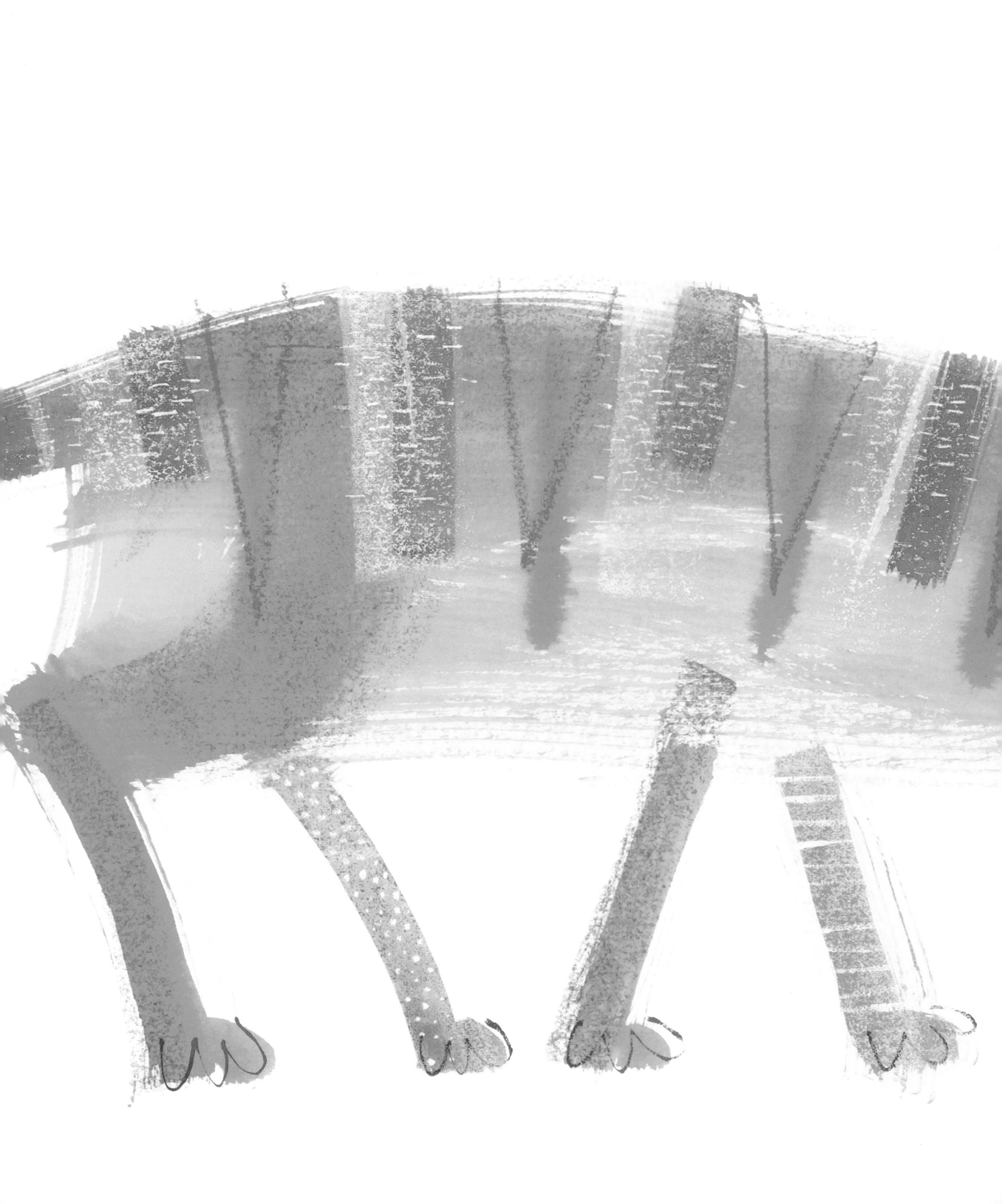

Curious

That snail just wants to talk,

But she speaks another language.

With no arms, she cannot sign…

So I'll just nod politely.

Hello?

Panic

Two big dogs just moved next door!

Slobbery, slathering kitty-eaters!

Maybe I'll hide behind the furnace.

My man says they're only poodles.

Gulp!

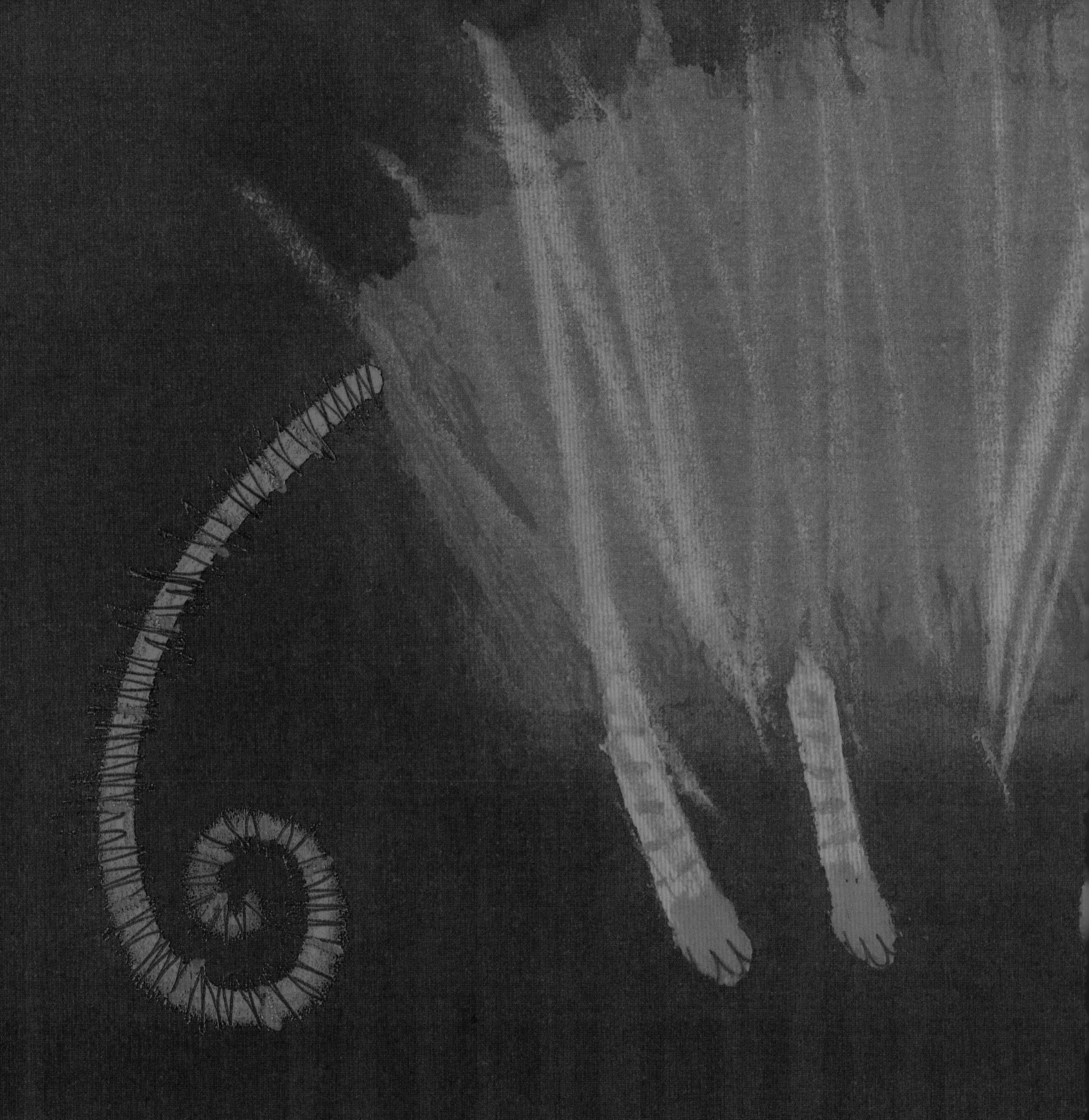

Sneaky

After my people are in their beds,
I'll have a sneaky fishbowl snack.
I'll drop the tail in Doggie's dish…
…He'll get no treats tomorrow.

Heh Heh!

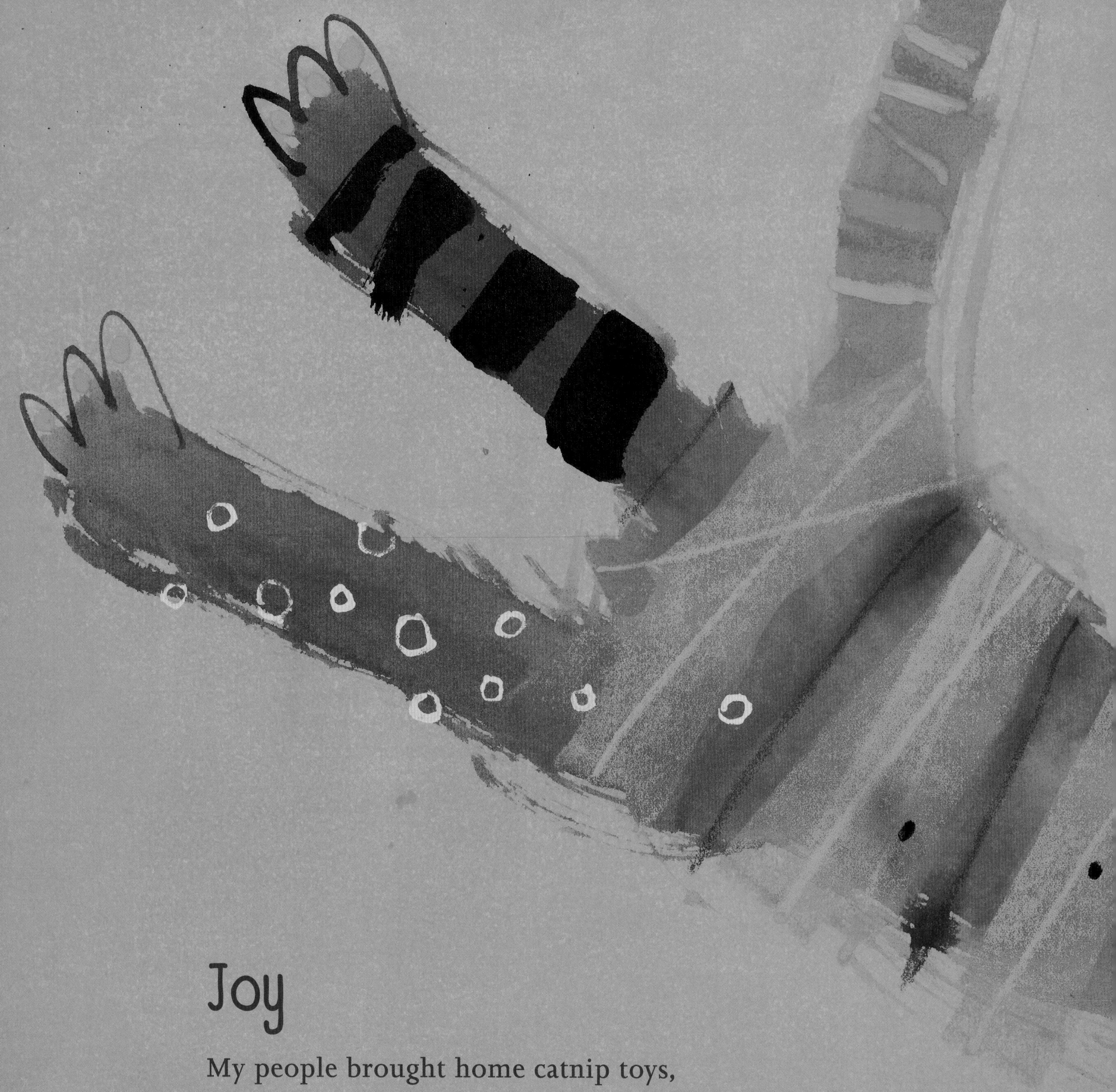

Joy

My people brought home catnip toys,
And now I am SOOO pleased!
Balls and bones and fluffy mice.
I'll roll around the floor some more.

Hee Hee!

Grandmother

I am the QUEEN of all the cats.
I have sixty-three grand-kitties.
I've forgotten almost all their names…
…but ALICE is the prettiest.

Smile.

Wash Time

Momma cleans behind my ears…

…the spots I cannot reach.

When I get big I'll clean myself,

So she can get some sleep!

Yep.

Princess

I am a spec-TAC-ular beauty...

...I LIVE to look in mirrors.

But I haven't any true-blue friends...

...I wonder why that is.

Frown.

Clever Tom

I am a stealthy alley cat.

I hunt fat mice at night.

I know where all the mean dogs live...

and where grannies put their pork-chop scraps.

Slink...

Warm

I like to curl up by the fire…

…and warm these tired old bones.

They say a cat has just nine lives,

But I have almost twenty!

Good night.

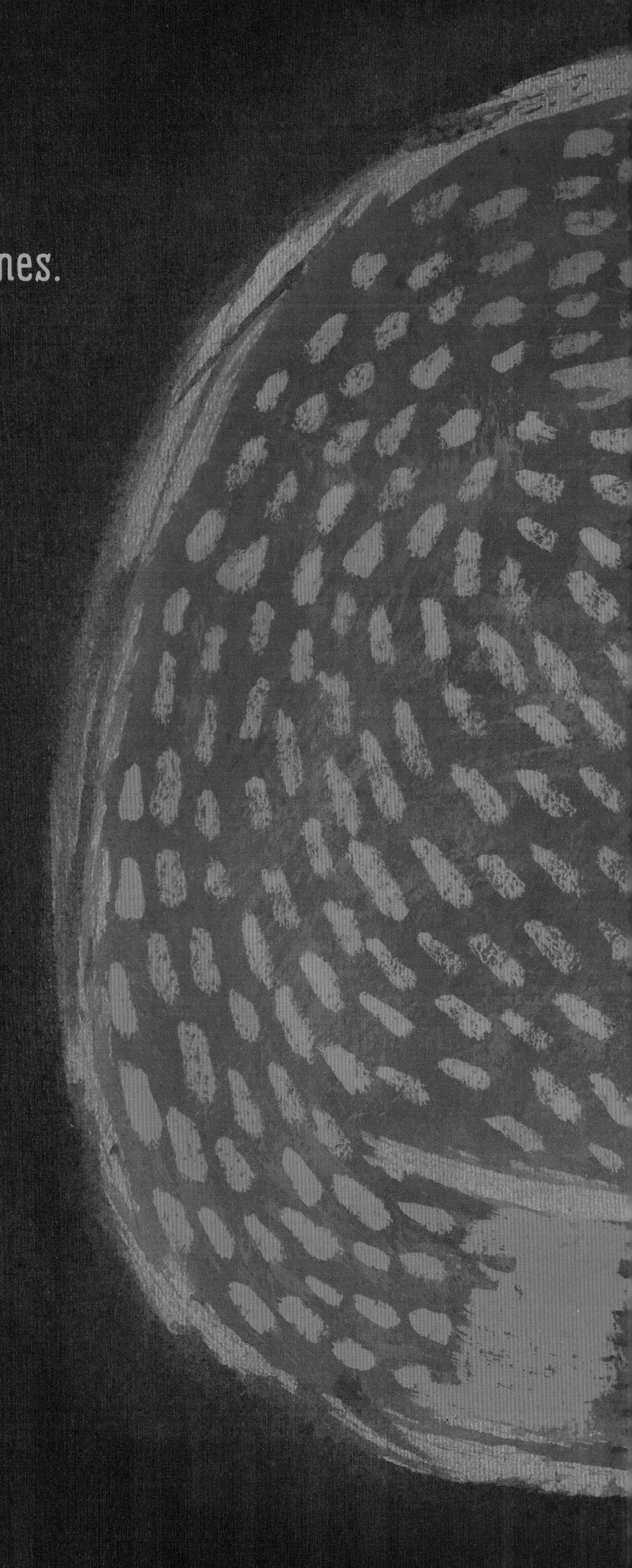

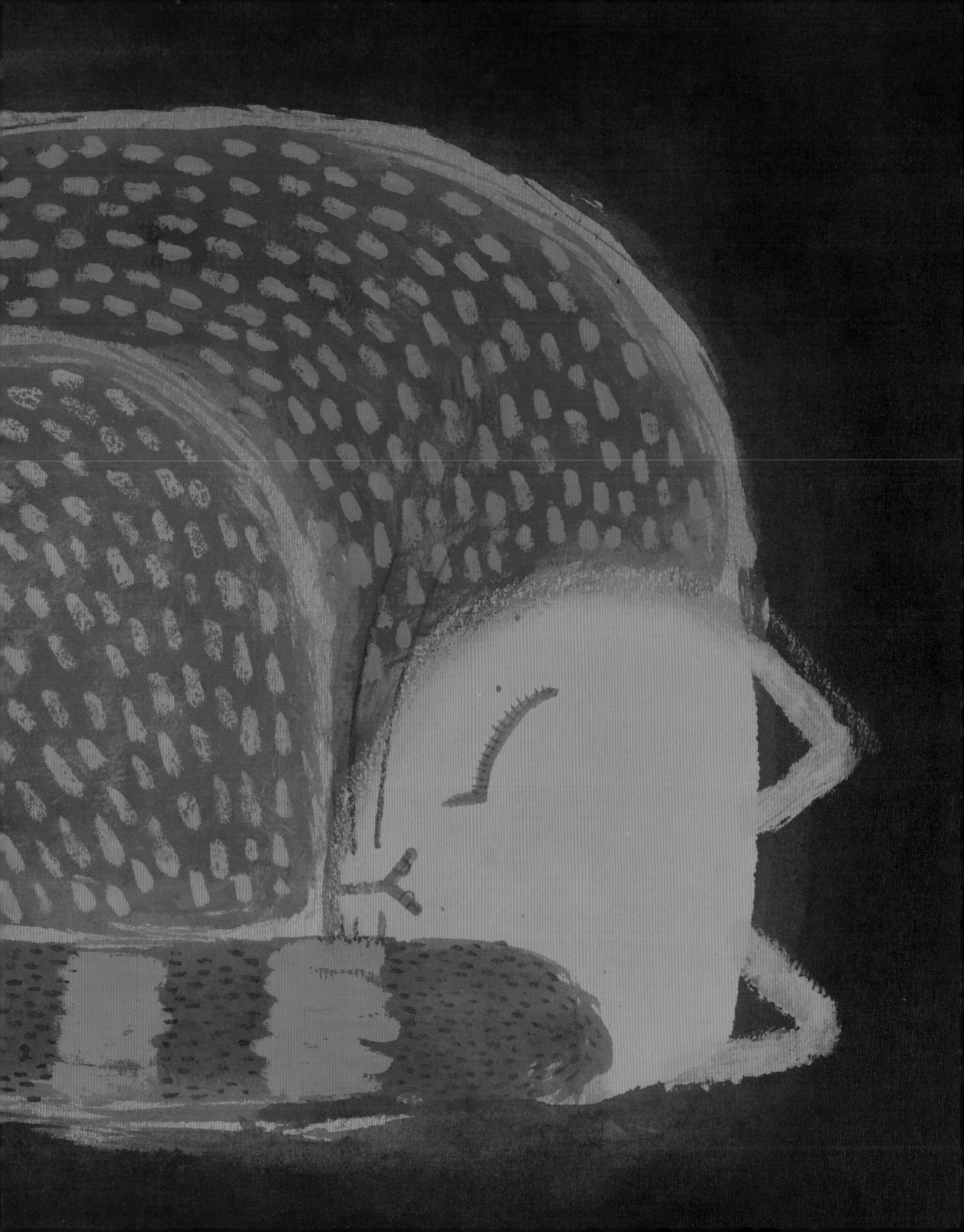

First published in Canada and the United States in 2019

Originally published by Uitgeverij Hoogland & Van Klaveren, Hoorn, the Netherlands under the title *Dag Poes!*
Adaptation rights arranged by élami agency

10 9 8 7 6 5 4 3 2 1

www.pajamapress.ca info@pajamapress.ca

Canada Council for the Arts Conseil des arts du Canada

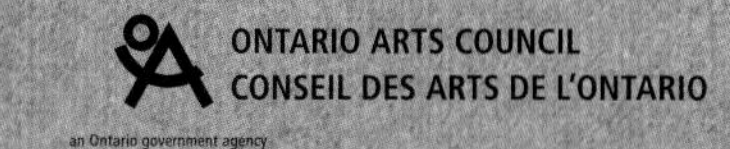

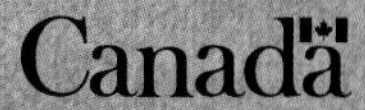

The publisher gratefully acknowledges the support of the Canada Council for the Arts and the Ontario Arts Council for its publishing program. We acknowledge the financial support of the Government of Canada through the Canada Book Fund (CBF) for our publishing activities.

Library and Archives Canada Cataloguing in Publication

Title: What cats think / Mies van Hout ; text by John Spray.
Other titles: Dag poes! English
Names: Hout, Mies van, artist. | Spray, John, 1948- author.
Description: "Originally published by Uitgeverij Hoogland & Van Klaveren, Hoorn, the Netherlands under the title Dag poes!"--Title page verso.
Identifiers: Canadiana 20190088311 | ISBN 9781772780871 (hardcover)
Classification: LCC PZ7.H8325 Wha 2019 | DDC j839.313/7

Publisher Cataloging-in-Publication Data (U.S.)

Names: Spray, John, 1948-, author. | Hout, Mies van, illustrator.
Title: What Cats Think / [illustrated by] Mies van Hout ; text by John Spray.
Description: Toronto, Ontario Canada : Pajama Press, 2019. | Originally published by Hoogland and Van Klaveren, Netherlands, 2017 as: Dag poes! | Summary: "Clever poetry and striking illustrations come together to celebrate the personalities of cats by depicting our feline companions in a variety of thoughtful and humorous"— Provided by publisher.
Identifiers: ISBN 978-1-77278-087-1 (hardcover)
Subjects: LCSH: Cats -- Juvenile poetry. | Personality – Juvenile poetry. | Humorous poetry. | BISAC: JUVENILE FICTION / Animals / Cats. | JUVENILE FICTION / Poetry. | JUVENILE FICTION / Humorous stories.
Classification: LCC PZ7.S673Wha |DDC [E] – dc23

Original art created with acrylic ink, oil pastels and gouache

Manufactured by Qualibre Inc./Print Plus
Printed in China

Pajama Press Inc.
181 Carlaw Ave. Suite 251 Toronto, Ontario Canada, M4M 2S1

Distributed in Canada by UTP Distribution
5201 Dufferin Street Toronto, Ontario Canada, M3H 5T8

Distributed in the U.S. by Ingram Publisher Services
1 Ingram Blvd. La Vergne, TN 37086, USA